AESOP'S FABLES

The Hare and the Tortoise

Adapted by Ronne Randall
Illustrated by Louise Gardner

p

Hare was the most boastful animal in the whole forest.

On this fine, sunny morning, he was trotting down the forest path singing, "I'm handsome and clever and the fastest hare ever! There's no one as splendid as me!"

Hedgehog, Mouse and Squirrel watched him from the fallen log.

"Hare is so annoying," said Hedgehog. "Someone should find a way to stop him boasting all the time!"

"I'll get him to stop!" said Squirrel and he jumped on to the path right in front of Hare. "I'm as handsome as you are, Hare," he said. "Look at my big bushy tail."

"It's not as handsome as my fluffy white tail and my long silky ears!" boasted Hare.

"Well, I'm as clever as you are!" said Mouse, hurrying out to join them. "I can dig holes under trees and store enough nuts and seeds to last all winter!"

"That's nothing!" said Hare. "In winter, I can change my coat to white, so that I can hide in the snow!"

"Now, is there anyone who thinks they can run as *fast* as me?" said Hare to the animals, who had gathered round. "Who wants a race?"

No one said anything! All the animals knew that Hare was *very fast* and no one thought they could beat him.

"Ha!" exclaimed Hare. "That proves it! I'm the handsomest, the cleverest *and* the fastest."

"Excuse me," said a small voice.

"Yes?" said Hare, turning around.

"I will race you," said Tortoise.

"YOU?" said Hare, in amazement. "The slowest, clumsiest animal on four legs?"

"Yes," said Tortoise, quietly. "I will race you."

The other animals gasped and Hare roared with laughter.

"Will you race me to the willow tree?" Hare asked Tortoise.

"Yes," said Tortoise.

"Will you race past the willow tree, to the stream?" asked Hare.

"Yes, I will," said Tortoise.

"Will you race past the willow tree, past the stream and all the way to the old oak tree?" asked Hare.

"Of course I will," said Tortoise.

"Fine," said Hare. "We'll start at nine o'clock in the morning! We'll meet right here, at the big oak tree."

"All right," said Tortoise.

The other animals ran off to tell their friends the news.

The next morning, the forest was buzzing with excitement. Everyone had turned out to watch the big race. Some were at the starting line and others were going to the finish, to see who would get there first.

Magpie called, "Ready, set, GO!"

And Tortoise and Hare were off!

Hare shot past Tortoise and the crowds and, when there was no one to show off for, he slowed down just a bit. He reached the willow tree and looked behind him – Tortoise was not in sight!

"It will take him ages just to catch me," Hare thought. "I don't need to hurry. I may as well stop and rest."

He sat down under the willow tree and closed his eyes. In minutes, he was fast asleep.

Meanwhile, Tortoise just plodded on.

He didn't try to go faster than he could, but he didn't stop, either. He just kept going, one foot in front of the other, on and on and on.

The sun climbed higher in the sky and Tortoise felt hot.

But he still kept going. His stubby legs were beginning to ache, but he knew he mustn't stop.

Hare just kept snoring under
the willow tree.

Some time later, Tortoise reached Hare, who was still fast asleep.

First of all, Tortoise thought he should wake Hare up. Then he changed his mind.

"Hare is very clever," he told himself. "He must have a reason for sleeping. He would only be angry if I woke him!"

So, Tortoise left Hare sleeping under the tree and went on his way, one foot in front of the other, walking slowly towards the finish line.

Later that afternoon, as the sun began to sink and the air grew chilly, Hare awoke with a start.

"The race!" he thought. "I *have* to finish the race!"

He looked around to see if Tortoise was nearby. There was no sign of him.

"Hah!" said Hare. "He still hasn't caught up with me. No need to hurry, then."

And he trotted towards the clearing, with a big grin on his face.

When he neared the finish, Hare could hear cheers and clapping.

"They must be able to see me coming," he thought.

But, as he got closer, he saw the real reason for all the noise and his heart sank.

There was Tortoise, crossing the line.

Tortoise had won!

The animals were cheering wildly.

As Hare crept up to the finishing
line, the cheers turned to laughter.
His ears turned bright red and drooped
with embarrassment.

Hare moped off and everyone gathered round to congratulate Tortoise, who looked shy, but very proud. He had proved that slow but steady always wins the race.

The animals smiled at one another. Somehow they knew that they wouldn't have to listen to Hare's loud, annoying boasting any more!